First published in Great Britain 2014 by Egmont UK Limited
This edition published 2019 by Dean, an imprint of Egmont UK Limited,
The Yellow Building, 1 Nicholas Road, London, W11 4AN
www.egmont.co.uk

Text copyright © Timothy Knapman 2014
Illustrations copyright © Russell Ayto 2014

The moral rights of the author and illustrator have been asserted.

ISBN 978 0 6035 7580 8

70180/002

Printed in Malaysia

A CIP catalogue record for this title is available from the British Library.

To Jonathan and Sebastian with love _ T.K.

For my Father . . . Christmas? _ R.A.

A VERY PIRATE CHRISTMAS

Timothy Knapman ✶ Russell Ayto

EGMONT

Once upon a Christmas night,

when children tried to sleep,

Santa Claus's magic sleigh swooped over the ocean deep.

His sack was full of presents,
and his heart was full of joy,
But just before he sighted land
he heard a strange "Ahoy!"

A crew of scurvy pirates were lurking in the dark,
Savage as a stormy sea
and greedy as a shark.

They climbed aboard that flying sleigh

and did a dreadful thing...

They tied poor
Father Christmas up

with
gift wrap
and
with string!

Then Eyepatch Jim, their captain,
put on Santa's famous suit.

He danced a pirate jig and sang,

The pirates took a while to learn to steer the magic sleigh:

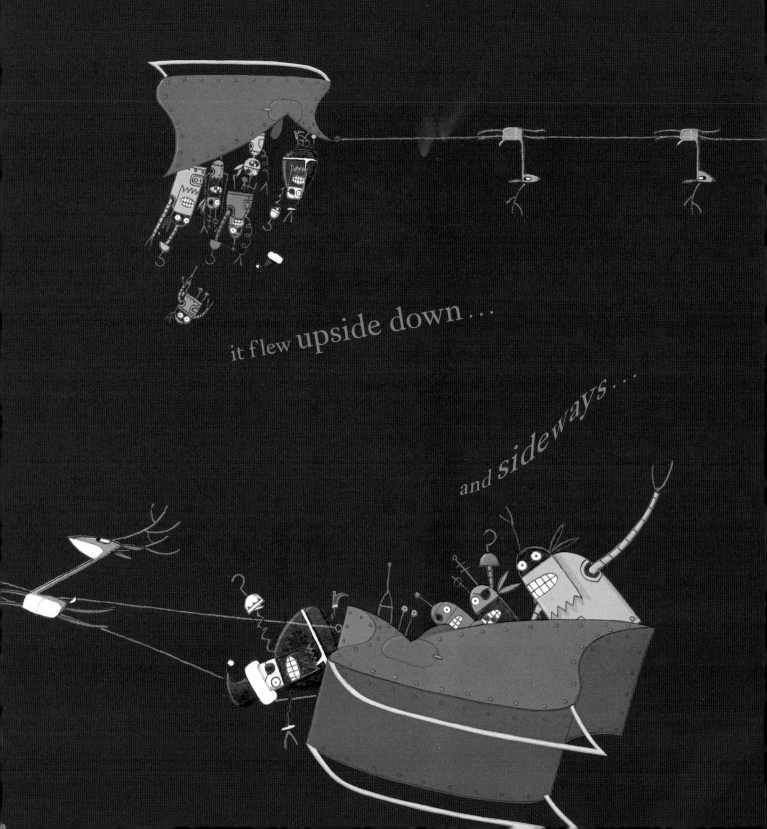

it flew **upside down** . . .

and *sideways* . . .

then completely the wrong way!

But – at last – they sorted out
the reindeer and the reins,

And, sighting land, great hopes of
greedy mischief filled their brains.

Those sea dogs hopped across the roofs,
dropped ropes down chimney stacks . . .

. . . and leaving salty footprints,
made their Christmas Eve attacks.

They took the tinsel and the trees,
the stars, the stockings too,

The turkeys and the puddings!
What a rotten thing to do!

They stole the whole of Christmas
and they kept it for themselves,
That no-good pirate Santa
and his wicked peg-leg elves.

And back aboard their ship they held
the roaring-est of parties –
a very **pirate** Christmas – cheering
"Yo ho ho, me hearties!

Look at us, we've plundered
every Christmas thing we could.
There's **nothing** for the children –
serves them right for being good!"

Across the world, all children slept
and dreamed of Christmas Day.

They didn't know that scurvy crew
had **stolen** it away.

All of them but **one**,
because that noisy

**Yo
ho
ho!**

Woke up **Pip** the cabin boy
who was sleeping down below.

He went on deck to shush them –
and what a shock he had.
He cried,

"You've stolen CHRISTMAS! How could you be SO BAD?"

But Eyepatch Jim said crossly,

"Don't you take that tone with me. GRAB him, lads, let's THROW this party pooper in the SEA!"

But they'd eaten too much turkey, too much pudding, too much cake,

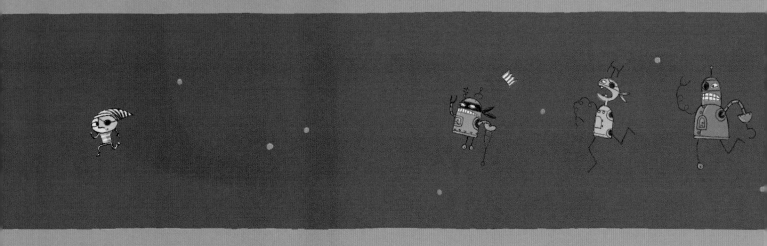

The pirates stopped, and coughed and wheezed.

And realised too late that chasing Pip was a mistake!

Their tummies were upset.

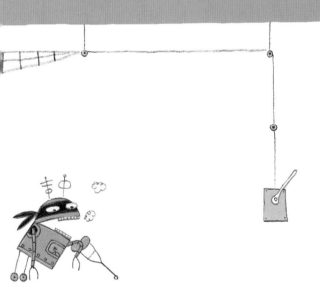

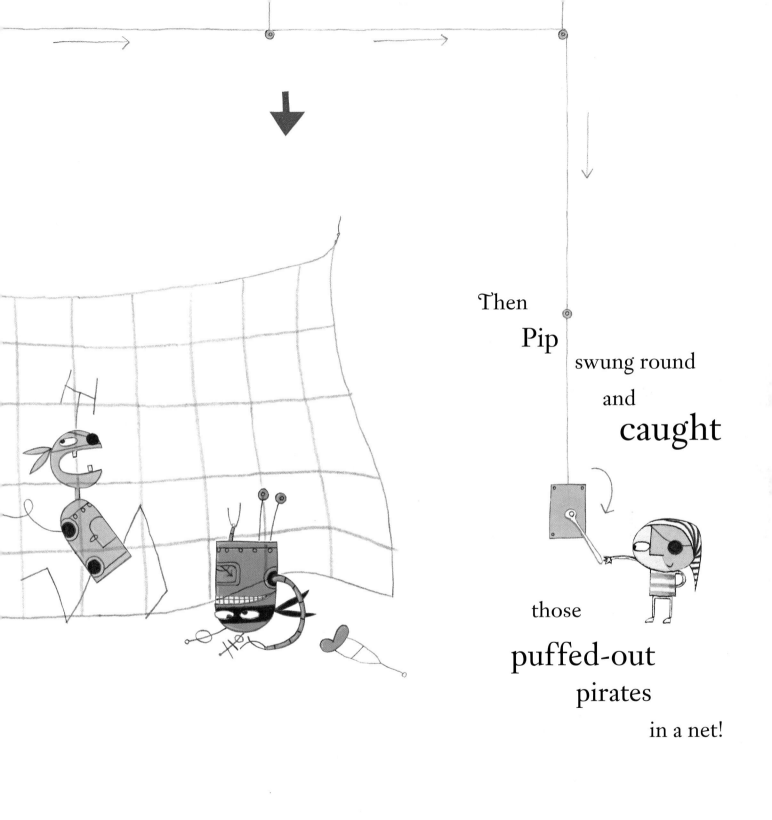

Then
Pip
swung round
and
caught

those

puffed-out
pirates
in a net!

Pip untied Santa Claus and only set the pirates free
Once they swore to put back Christmas – every present, every tree.

"For saving me, and Christmas," said Santa Claus to Pip,
"You get this Christmas present: you're now **captain of this ship!**

And as for naughty Eyepatch Jim, well, if I had to choose,
I'd say make *him* the cabin boy – and make him scrub the loos!"

So at top speed, and grumbling,
the pirates crossed the world
Returning **stolen** Christmas joy
to sleeping boys and girls.

And just in time they got it done so no one ever knew
About that **very** **pirate** Christmas . . .

. . . no one, that is,
but you!